For Tony DT, who loves creepies and crawlies of all kinds, and for Angela DT, who doesn't —JY

For Caroline and Amelia, who love some bugs, others not so much —JS

The publisher thanks John L. Capinera, PhD, chairman of the Entomology Department
at the University of Florida, for reviewing the text and photographs for this book.
The author and photographer thank Andy Boyles, science editor at Boyds Mills Press,
for his good advice and careful eye.

Front cover: golden silk orbweaver;
Front flap: flesh fly;
Back cover: deer fly;
Page 1: leaffooted bug;
Pages 2–3: black swallowtail caterpillar;
Page 4: black-tailed red sheetweaver;
Page 32: carpenter bee.

WORD/ONG

An Imprint of Boyds Mills Press, Inc.
815 Church Street
Honesdale, Pennsylvania 18431
Printed in China

ISBN: 978-1-59078-862-2
Library of Congress Control Number: 2011939947

First edition
The text of this book is set in Sabon.
10 9 8 7 6 5 4 3